Believing is just the beginning...

This magical
Annual belongs to

....

TinkerBell

Annual 2011

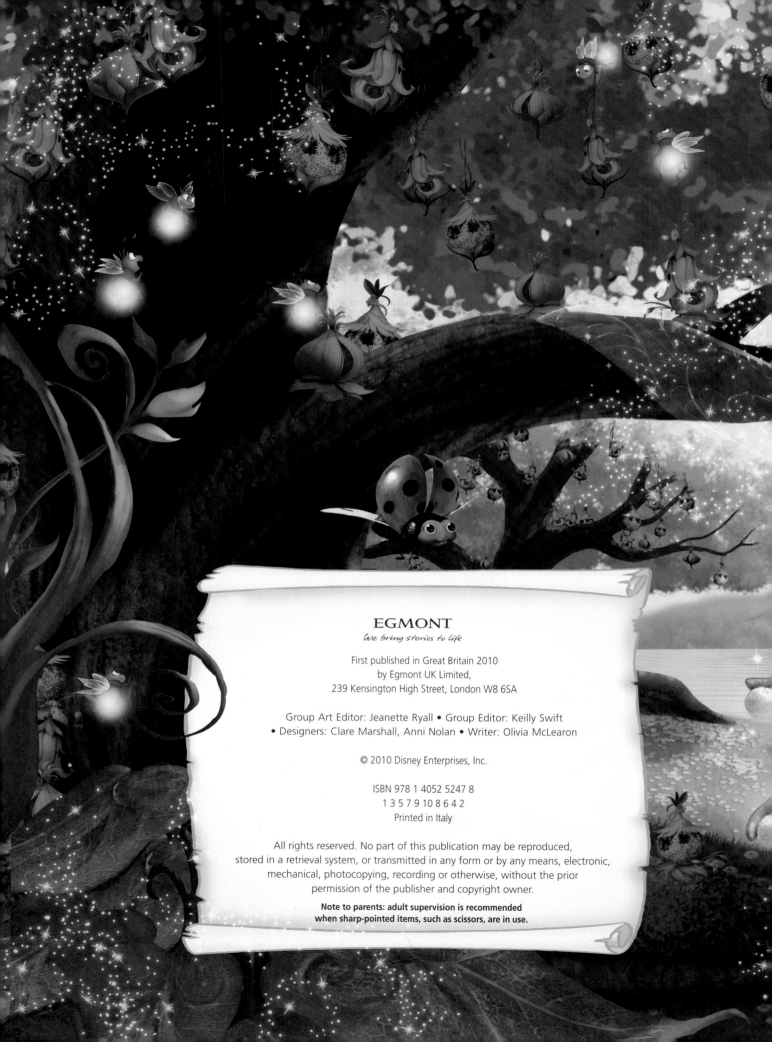

EGMONT

We bring stories to life

First published in Great Britain 2010
by Egmont UK Limited,
239 Kensington High Street, London W8 6SA

Group Art Editor: Jeanette Ryall • Group Editor: Keilly Swift
• Designers: Clare Marshall, Anni Nolan • Writer: Olivia McLearon

© 2010 Disney Enterprises, Inc.

ISBN 978 1 4052 5247 8
1 3 5 7 9 10 8 6 4 2
Printed in Italy

**Note to parents: adult supervision is recommended
when sharp-pointed items, such as scissors, are in use.**

Discover all this inside!

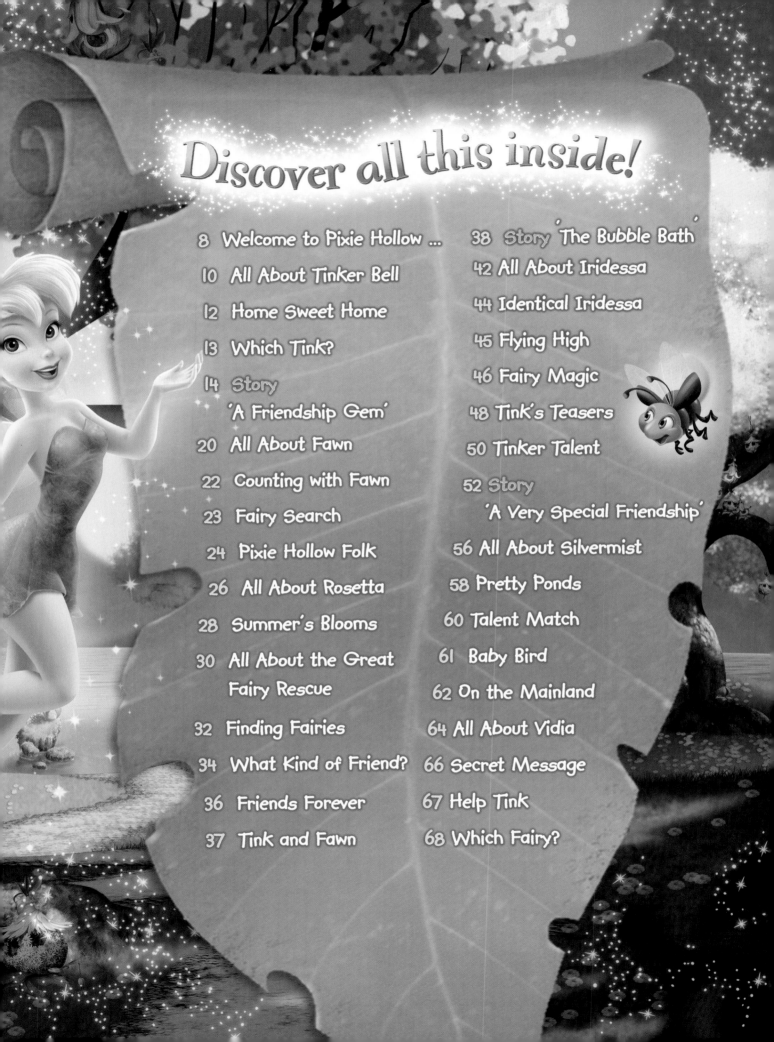

Welcome to Pixie Hollow...

Pixie Hollow is a magical place, on an island called Never Land. It is home to a host of fairies, including Tinker Bell, Rosetta, Silvermist, Fawn, Iridessa and Vidia. Each of the fairies has their own particular talent, the thing that they are best at.

Never Land

Tinker Bell is charming, lovable and determined. She is a tinker fairy, talented at mending broken pots, pans and other objects.

Iridessa
likes everything to be perfect in every way and is fiercely loyal. She is a light fairy who can bend, shape and create illumination.

Fawn
is a total tomboy, who's full of mischief! She is an animal fairy who can understand and speak to all creatures.

Rosetta
is sweet, funny, and always likes to look her best. She is a garden fairy who cares for the flowers of Pixie Hollow.

Silvermist
is friendly, caring and optimistic. She is a water fairy and can move and control water.

Vidia
likes her own company and isn't very friendly. But she has a secret soft side. Her talent is being the fastest flying fairy around.

Tinker Bell
All about your fairy friend . . .

Fairy talent:
Pots and Kettles Fairy

Fairy task:
to repair broken pots,
pans and kettles

Lives in:
a tea kettle,
Sparkling Valley

Character:
feisty, fun-loving and
kind-hearted

Talent icon:
hammer

Use your brightest crayons or felt-tips to bring this pretty picture of Tinker Bell to life.

Count: How many butterflies can you see in this picture? Write your answer in the box.

Answer: there are 5 butterflies.

Home Sweet Home

This is Tinker Bell's home in Tinkers' Nook. Which pieces are missing from the jigsaw picture? See if you can work it out using the four choices below!

Answer: pieces C and D are missing.

12

Which Tink?

These five pictures of Tinker Bell all look identical, but there is one that is different. Can you spot it? Write your answer in the box.

Tink number ⬚ is the odd one out!

13

A Friendship Gem

Oooh, what's that?

Tinker Bell loves looking for lost things.

Tink comes up with an invention to help her catch the sparkly thing.

I did it! Hooray!

It's such a beautiful, err . . . thing!

Tink takes the sparkly thing to Fairy Mary to see if she knows what it is.

It's a gem! Each one offers a different gift and the gem decides who will find it.

Wow!

Tink can't wait to make the gem sparkle again and discover the gem's gift.

Don't worry, Fairy Mary, I'll make it sparkle again!

Tink makes a special brush to clean the gem.

Great! That'll do it!

But the brush doesn't work . . .

. . . and the gem just gets smaller.

But, why is it getting smaller?

Tink goes to see Fawn to see if she can help her make the gem sparkle.

Try this fluffy feather!

But the gem just gets even smaller . . .

. . . and smaller.

Tinker Bell and Fawn decide to find Silvermist to see if she can help.

Tink explains the story of the gem to Silvermist and asks if she has any ideas for cleaning the gem.

Leave it to me.

Silvermist asks Tink to place the gem right beside the river.

I'll polish it with a little wave!

Tink is determined to make her gem sparkle.

Let's see if Iridessa or Rosetta can help.

But the water doesn't work and the gem becomes even smaller.

But neither Iridessa's sunbeam . . .

. . . nor Rosetta's berry juice does the trick.

Nothing seems to work!

It's just so tiny!

Fawn
All about your fairy friend . . .

Fairy talent:
Animal Fairy

Fairy task:
to understand, help and
speak to all creatures

Lives in:
a pine cone, Pine Forest

Character:
energetic, playful tomboy

Talent icon:
bird's egg

Colour:
Use your favourite pens to add some magical colours to this picture!

Counting with Fawn

Fawn is counting some of the creatures in Pixie Hollow.
Count how many of each animal there are, then
write your answers in the boxes.

Fireflies   **Fishes**   **Frogs**   **Birds**   **Ladybugs**

Fairy Search

Help Tinker Bell find these names in the grid.
They're hidden across and down. We've filled
one in to help you and Tink out!

Rosetta

Silvermist

Vidia

Clank

Iridessa

Fawn

Fairy Mary

Bobble

Terence

```
S  F  A  I  R  Y  M  A  R  Y
I  R  I  D  E  S  S  A  C  T
L  O  S  L  B  A  F  Y  T  K
V  B  C  R  O  S  E  T  T  A
E  T  N  I  R  A  I  W  B  C
R  S  B  O  B  B  L  E  C  V
M  G  U  E  O  M  N  P  T  I
I  F  A  W  N  C  L  A  L  D
S  H  T  E  R  E  N  C  E  I
T  C  L  A  N  K  J  D  F  A
```

Pixie Hollow Folk

Pixie Hollow is a magical place, with hundreds of different fairies who live and work there. Each fairy is unique and has their own special job to do.

The Ministers

The Ministers of the seasons and their fairies work together to change every seasonal detail, at the start of each season. They're also in charge of leading their fairies to the Mainland.

Frost Fairies

They look as delicate as snowflakes, but the frost fairies are tough cookies! They have to be, because led by the Minister of Winter, they help bring winter to the Mainland.

Sparrowmen

Sparrowmen are male fairies. Tink's friend Terence is a sparrowman. Just like female fairies, they all have different talents. Clank and Bobble are tinker sparrowmen who work with Tink.

Fairy Mary

Fairy Mary is the fairies' headteacher and a teaching talent fairy. She is very caring, but worries a lot in case her fairies do the wrong thing!

Rosetta

All about your fairy friend . . .

Fairy talent:
Garden Fairy

Fairy task:
cares for all the plants
and flowers in Pixie Hollow

Lives in:
a house made from daisies,
Buttercup Canyon

Character:
generous, caring and dramatic

Talent icon:
flower

Use your brightest pens
to colour in this beautiful
picture of Rosetta.

Draw:
Sketch your favourite
flower here.

27

Summer's Blooms

It's summertime in Pixie Hollow, so Tink is helping her friend, Rosetta the Garden Fairy, paint these pretty pink blooms.

Draw over the outlines, using your prettiest pens, then colour them in.

29

All About the Great Fairy Rescue

The fairies travel to the Mainland for the start of summer in the Great Fairy Rescue, and find all kinds of scares and excitement there!

Fairy Camps

Bringing the change to summer takes a lot of hard work and massive sprinkles of pixie dust. This means that the fairies have to set up fairy camps.

Fairy Fall-out

One day, Tink annoys Vidia, by showering her with water by mistake. Vidia is upset when her revenge results in Tink being kidnapped by a girl named Lizzy.

Saving Tink

The fairies, led by Vidia, come to Tink's rescue! The fearless five prove that all you need for a fab fairy friendship is faith, trust and pixie dust!

Vidia

Vidia proves that a fairy really can change. A much nicer side of her emerges – a side that she normally keeps hidden!

Finding Fairies

See if you can help Vidia spot her fairy friends, flying creatures and the pretty flowers hidden around the pond.

How many ladybugs are there on the page?

Unscramble the letters to find a special word.

Can you tell which fairy is hiding behind the flower at the top?

Tick the boxes when you see these fairies and creatures in the picture.

What Kind of Friend?

Tink and her friends are wonderful in so many different ways. Which one are you most like?

Heart of gold

Which fairy is she?
Silvermist

Special friendship ability:
being a fantastic listener.

You're like her if:
you're always there for your friends.

Happy helper

Which fairy is she?
Iridessa

Special friendship ability:
helping friends out in their hour of need.

You're like her if:
you're very organised and super helpful.

Sweet soul

Which fairy is she?
Rosetta

Special friendship ability:
giving brilliant, honest advice.

You're like her if:
your friends always ask you what you think.

Funny friend

Which fairy is she?
Tink

Special friendship ability:
making someone who's sad laugh with joy.

You're like her if:
you're fiercely loyal and always cheer your friends up.

Playful pal

Which fairy is she?
Fawn

Special friendship ability:
being tons of fun!

You're like her if:
you love playing games with your friends.

Write which fairy you are most like:

. . . .

My best friend is most like:

. . . .

Friends Forever

Sometimes you find friends in the most unexpected places . . .

In times of upset and trouble,
When you just don't know what to do,
It could be the person you least expect,
Who'll stop you feeling blue.

❋

There for you through good times and bad,
For the giggles, as well as the tears,
They listen to you and give you advice,
And help you get over your fears.

❋

Some offer sympathy, others are fun,
Friends bring joy in so many ways,
They light up our lives with laughter,
There for you each and every day.

Tink and Fawn

These two pictures might look the same, but there are five differences in picture b. See if you can find them all.

a

b

Colour in a flower every time you find a difference.

Answers: In picture b - Fawn's top is a different colour, the ladybug is blue, a pink flower has vanished, a ladybug has disappeared and a pink butterfly has gone.

The Bubble Bath

Tinker Bell has found a new lost thing. She wants to use it to make a surprise for Fawn . . .

That's a wonderful idea, Sweet Pea!

Hmmm . . .

Fawn will be so happy!

Morning, Fairy Mary!

What are you doing with that TEACUP?

We are going to turn it into a BATH CUP for the birds!

Oh!

Let's get to work, girls!

You can't take a bath without **WATER**!

Wow! These bubbles are great, Sil!

Rosetta adds a floral touch . . .

MMM, that smells nice!

Thanks! Now it's a **FLITTERIFIC** bath cup!

39

Then, when Rosetta and Silvermist fly off . . .

Where are you going to put the cup?

I'll leave it HERE in Sunflower Meadow!

Oh. . . . interesting!

So Fawn's little bird friends can use it to keep their feet nice and cool!

I'm going to call FAWN!

Yes . . . um . . . of course! Go right ahead, dear!

Later on . . .

You're going to love my surprise! You'll see!

I'm sure I will!

But . . .

GASP! What's going on?

The End

Iridessa
All about your fairy friend ...

Fairy talent:
Light Fairy

Fairy task:
shapes, bends and creates light

Lives in:
a sunflower, Morning
Glow Meadow

Character:
intelligent, hardworking
and loyal

Talent icon:
glow ball

Use your most colourful pens to finish this lovely picture of Iridessa.

Count:
How many fireflies can you spot on these two pages?

There are ___ fireflies.

Identical Iridessa

Only two of these pictures of clever Iridessa are identical. Can you spot which two they are?

Flying High

Tink and Blaze need to get to the balloon. See if you can guide them through the maze!

Finish

Start

Fairy Magic

Discover all about the magical world of Pixie Hollow, where Tink and her friends live.

Arrival Day

A fairy is born each time a baby first laughs. The laugh then floats to Pixie Hollow on a fluff of dandelion. When it arrives, Queen Clarion and her fairies are waiting for it with a bundle of kindness and a big sprinkling of pixie dust.

Pixie Dust

Once the pixie dust is scattered over the dandelion wisp, the fairy comes alive. The fairies are given fresh pixie dust every day, as it helps them to make the most of their talent. Clever fairies can help others fly when they sprinkle them with pixie dust as well.

Finding the Talent

Each fairy has a special talent. When a new fairy is born, they're shown a collection of items and the one that shines the brightest becomes their talent icon. Tink's hammer really glowed when she first walked towards it! It also tells them where they'll live within Pixie Hollow.

Special Fairies

There are special Pixie Dust fairies who work at the Dust Distribution Depot, which is run by Fairy Gary. Tink's good friend Terence works there too. They have to make sure that there's enough pixie dust to go around, which is one cup per fairy per day.

My special talent

What would your special talent be? Write about it here and draw a picture of your talent icon beside it!

....

....

Tink's Teasers

Can you help Tink and her friends
with these puzzles?

Pixie Power

See if you can work
out which fairy is
hidden in the pixie dus

Odd Fawn Out

Which picture
of Fawn is the
odd one out?

A

B

C

D

E

48

Fairy Puzzler

Which fairy do these four parts belong to?

1

2

3

4

Talent Time

Cross out all of the letters that appear more than once to reveal Rosetta's talent icon.

A B G G F H
Q M S S L M B
A H P S T O U
P A W T Q B
Z E Y M Q T
R U P S Z Y

Tinker Talent

Do you have a Tinker talent? Choose between A and B to find out.

1 What can broken twigs be used for?

A. For birds to build nests.

B. To write your name out!

2 You break your pencil, so . . .

A. You buy a new one!

B. You tape it back together.

3 What do you do with old Christmas cards?

A. Recycle them.

B. Use them to make next year's Christmas cards!

4 Your favourite T-shirt has a hole in it . . .

A. You put it in the drawer and forget about it.

B. You patch it up with a flower design and it's brand-new again!

5 You find a chipped cup . . .

A. You put it away. Maybe you're the one who did it!

B. You turn it into a vase for a miniature plant!

Mostly As

Tinker talent? Not quite!

You're not interested in fiddling around with things that are broken or seem useless, but that's OK! Everyone has a natural talent. What's yours? It's something you're really good at and love doing!

Terrific tinker!

You're good at fixing, as well as making things, and would be a fantastic assistant for Tinker Bell. You love re-using objects that most people would throw out!

A Very Special Friendship

Rosetta, a Garden Fairy, is busy working with her talent!

The time to bloom is here!

. . . bloom!

And slowly but surely. . .

. . . all of the flowers bloom!

Well, almost all of them!

Why haven't you blossomed?

Bloom! Bloom! Bloom!

It's no use!

Need a hand, Rosetta?

I can't get it to blossom, Silvermist!

Maybe the flower just needs a little time, or . . . hey, look!

. . . the flower seems to have a friend down here!

It isn't blooming because of the fish?

Not exactly, Rosetta!

Get ready to use your talent!

Ok . . .

Little fish, are you ready to fly inside a bubble?

Now, Rosetta! Do your thing!

With pleasure!

It's time to bloom!

It's working . . . the flower starts to bloom!

The flower wanted its little friend, the fish, to be able to see it blossom!

Naturally!

They're so cute . . .

. . . in fact, they're the nicest pair of friends I've ever seen!

The End

Silvermist
All about your fairy friend ...

Fairy talent:
Water Fairy

Fairy task:
to control, move and manipulate water

Lives in:
a water lily in Stillwater Springs

Character:
friendly, calm and trusting

Talent icon:
water droplet

Make Silvermist shine even more by colouring her in with your pencils and felt tips.

Colour:
Add gorgeous colour to Silvermist and her lily pad!

Pretty Ponds

Can you and Fawn reach Silvermist
on the other side of the pond?

How to play

• You need a dice and a
counter for each player.
• Place all of the counters
at the start of the game.
• Take it in turns to throw the
dice and move across the pond.
• Make sure you follow the
instructions on the
lily pads!

5

4
Cheeky Fawn's splashed
you! Go back 1.

3

2
You've been given some
pixie dust! Go on 3.

1

Start

Talent Match

Each of the fairies in Pixie Hollow has their own talent.
Can you help Rosetta match her friends to their
talent icon? Draw a line to match them up.

1

2

3

4

5

A

B

C

D

E

Answers: 1 = B, 2 = D, 3 = C, 4 = A, 5 = E.

Baby Bird

Fawn's little bird friend has just hatched an egg. Can you help them both find the missing piece of his eggshell?

1

2

3

4

5

A

On the Mainland

The fairies journey to the Mainland at the start of every season and take care of all of the tiny details that bring about a new season . . .

Spring

The fairies all work together to make spring as stunning as possible. Rosetta makes the flowers blossom, while Tink's flower sprayer paints the spring flowers!

Summer

Changing spring to summer is hard work and needs lots of pixie dust. Iridessa makes the sun shine brighter and Silvermist encourages waters to gently ripple.

Autumn

The beautiful autumn leaves in the parks are a result of the hard work of the nature fairies. The wind? That's Vidia of course!

Winter

Snow is falling. It's winter! So, caring Fawn makes sure all of her woodland friends are safely hibernating.

Talented Tink

Clever Tink has invented things to help with the season change, so she's allowed to travel to the Mainland with the nature fairies, during the change of the seasons.

Vidia

All about your fairy friend ...

Fairy talent:
Fast-flying Fairy

Fairy task:
to make the wind blow

Lives in:
Sour Plum Tree

Character:
impatient and ambitious, but
deep down she's caring

Talent icon:
whirlwind

Use your most colourful pens to bring this lovely picture of Vidia to life.

Count:
Count how many pink butterflies there are on these two pages!

There are ⬜ butterflies.

Answer: there are 7 butterflies.

Secret Message

Tink wants to pass a message on to Vidia, but it's in code. Use the code breaker below to help Vidia work out what the message says.

A	B	C	D	E	F	G	H	I	J	K	L	M
✿	♠	▲	★	✿	◆	◎	◆	✚	✳	➡	■	❈

N	O	P	Q	R	S	T	U	V	W	X	Y	Z
✚	●	❄	⬗	♥	◖	✺	▮	▶	❓	☙	✳	○

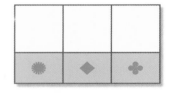

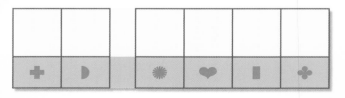

Help Tink

Vidia's sneaked into Tink's workshop and made a real mess. Help Tink search for the missing items below and tick each one off as you find it.

Which Fairy?

Which one of Tink's friends are you most like? Take our quiz and find out!

1

Your friends always come to you for . . .

a. Advice
b. Help
c. Games
d. Sympathy

2

You love . . .
a. Anything pretty
b. Being the best
c. Animals
d. Making your friends happy

3

Your favourite colour is . . .

a. Red
b. Yellow
c. Green
d. Blue

4

You get annoyed when . . .
a. You don't look your best
b. Things don't go according to plan
c. People take things too seriously
d. Friends fall out

5

If you were an animal, you would be . . .
a. A cute rabbit
b. A cool cat
c. A cheeky monkey
d. A graceful deer

Rosetta

Mostly A . . .
You love to look nice, just like **Rosetta**! You're also generous and caring.

Iridessa

Mostly B . . .
You're brainy and brilliant, like **Iridessa**. You like to be right, and you usually are!

Fawn

Mostly C . . .
You love games and having fun outside. You're animal mad, like **Fawn**!

Silvermist

Mostly D . . .
You're warm, friendly an kind. Like **Silvermist**, yo hate it when friends argu